First Love Revisited

The Wanderer of New Perry

Francine Carrière

First Love Revisited (short story)
The Wanderer of New Perry (romance)
Translated from *Comme un conte d'enfant/Le Clochard de New Perry* © 2012
by the author

Carrière, Francine — 1949-
Copyright © 2013 Francine Carrière
Website: francinecarriere.net
Distribution: www.amazon.ca
Illustrations: Lacombe, Martin —1980-
Copyright © 2011 Martin Lacombe
Setting: Richard Carrière — 1955-
Printing: www.ardith.ca
Manager of Publishing Services: Linda Palmer

Preface

I was fourteen when I wrote my first book: **"I Hate Men"**. I never finished it. I do not know what happened to it. When I say *Men*, I mean people in general.

I am dyslexic. I cannot write without making mistakes. It is very frustrating.

When I was twenty-five, I asked my little brother, Richard, to teach me French grammar.

In 1990, Richard told me about a contest for amateur writers. The first prize was $500 and the contestant would see his/her book published. 'You should participate,' he said. I wrote my romance, but I did not win. Thank God—I would have lost the copyright! My books are like my children: I cannot part with them.

In the movie *Remember Mama,* a mother asks a famous author: 'What advice do you have for my daughter?' The author answers: 'Tell her to write what she knows best.'

I am only interested in two subjects: breastfeeding and sexuality. Breastfeeding made me discover my feminine body. Passionate love has made me shiver with desire.

This book contains the short story that I wrote for the contest in 1990: *First Love Revisited.*

When I wrote this book, I was Sleeping Beauty, waiting to be kissed by my Prince.

Now I am Cinderella. I hope that, one day, my Prince riding his white horse will come to my work to sweep me away.

Since I can only write short stories, I have included my seventh work, a novel (2003) *The Wanderer of New Perry.*

Summary:

First Love Revisited— Fanny is in Toronto for a conference that happens to be given by her first boyfriend. The last day he invites her to his room. Both are married with children.

The Wanderer of New Perry. A woman saves the life of a man and tries to make him fall in love with her.

Who am I?

People say that I am 'bold, sensual, and passionate'. They also say that I have a lot of imagination. I have a strong maternal instinct.

In my next book you will find my second writing (1992) titled *The Enchanted Forest*, and my fourth (2000): *ATOM on the Blue Planet*.

Coming soon: *The Bet* (2010).

With LLLove,*
Francine Carrière

....

* The three LLL are to salute La Leche League with gratitude. They encouraged me to listen to my maternal instinct by breastfeeding, loving, respecting, and guiding my children to become responsible adults.

First Love Revisited

Thank you, R. B. M.
I am starting to like myself better.
1985

Special thanks to my brother Richard for his patience teaching me
'ba-be-bi-bo-bus'.

Thank you also, Claudette H.

CHAPTER I

'Hello, yes, it's me. Well, if it isn't the phantom of my past!' cries Fanny. 'Yes, of course. Give me forty-five minutes.'

Fanny puts the telephone down and shouts with joy.

'My God! I don't have any time to lose!'

She runs to her closet. This blue dress, yes, it has to be blue! As for the banquet Saturday night, she will have to wear something else.

Fanny Cadieux-Millaire is forty years old with blond hair, thanks to those little boxes of hair dye that help cover the grey. She is five feet and three inches tall. Her green eyes, which at times change to blue, make her look charming. With exercise and a good diet she manages to stay in pretty good shape.

She is not pretty, but with good make-up she can make herself look presentable. They say that women are pretty at that age and Fanny comes close to it.

Fanny is a very good mother; she left her job years ago in order to raise her children. She is also a faithful wife, putting her family first. Now that the children are older she has decided to return to school to study Child Psychology.

She is in Toronto for a week. She has registered for a seminar which is given, in part, by the famous psychologist Roch Bernard Maisonneuve.

"Oh my God! I will never be ready in time. A shower, make-up! No, calm down or you are never going to make it."

She calms herself and gets into the shower. While the water is running, she takes a good look at her body. How is she at forty? Slowly, she caresses her breasts, she is so proud of them. She should be, has she not breastfed her five children?

She puts her make-up on, slips on her blue dress and, after a sigh of relief, she opens the door of her hotel room.

In the elevator, she recalls their first meeting twenty-three years ago.

'You're not skating?'

'No, I don't have skates.'

She turned to see who was talking. It was a very young, handsome man with black hair, green eyes, and the most wonderful smile. She timidly smiled at him and then turned back to look at the children playing on the skating rink.

'It's too bad. You don't know what you're missing,' he replied while putting his skates on and then he ran onto the ice to join his friends for a hockey match.

When he asked her if she would join him for a hot chocolate, she accepted. A hot chocolate seemed so good especially in that cold.

She remembers that day just like it was yesterday—the aroma of the chocolate, the warmth she feels while drinking it. The thought of it makes her shiver. The door of the elevator opens … he is there!

Before stepping out she looks at him. He is still very elegant, almost the same except for a little touch of white in his black hair.

Before he can see her, she is in front of him.

'Hello, Mr. Maisonneuve,' she says extending her hand to welcome him. 'I am Fanny Cadieux-Millaire.'

He turns to look at her. She is still pretty! For a moment, he stands still, astonished, then he regains his composure and shakes her hand. Without hesitation he promptly guides her out of the hotel.

Always a gentleman, he opens the door for her, taking the opportunity to admire her beautiful legs. She's still got it!

For a moment, Fanny has second thoughts. What is she doing? What is she getting into? She should excuse herself and return to the hotel!

But it's too late; Roch has started the car and is smiling at her.

Ah! why worry! Tonight all she cares is to be is a woman— if only her heart could stop beating so hard and her voice stop shaking.

CHAPTER II

They have found a restaurant not too far from the hotel, sitting in front of each other—he drinking coffee and her a hot chocolate.

She shivers because she was never at ease with him. That is why she lets him talk first.

'How many children do you have?' he asks her.

'I have five children, four girls and one boy.'

'I'm not surprise. You always loved children.'

With a napkin he dries his lips and then says, 'Do you still live in New Perry?'

'Yes, New Perry is our hometown. And since we are family oriented, Emile and I have chosen to raise our children there.'

Surprised he spills a bit of his coffee and shouts, 'You're married to Emile Millaire?'

'Yes, he's a nice guy and a good father.'

'I'm sure about that. At school my friends used to tease me. They said that if I wasn't careful, Emile would take you away from me. He always had the hots for you.'

He takes two sips of his coffee and adds, 'He was always a nice guy.'

In between sips Fanny asks him, 'How many children do you have?'

'I have two, a boy and a girl.'

They talk about the weather, things that people do to pass the time.

Suddenly, he questions her, 'Do you still like to go for long walks? Do you remember when we used to walk on the beach for hours on end?'

'Yes, I remember,' she replies. 'Why are you asking me that?'

'Because I would like to show you around Toronto, if that interests you.'

'Why not, I'd be glad to walk with you.'

'Make sure you wear good shoes. I'll meet you in the lobby tomorrow morning at eight o'clock."

The next morning, dressed in a jean skirt and a pink blouse, Fanny waits for Roch.

She almost faints when she sees him; he is wearing a pair of jeans and his pink shirt is unbuttoned, enough to show the hair on his chest. Fanny likes hairy chests.

'My God! I am done!'

She takes one step to join him and then stops.

No, she wishes it wasn't true! After all these years he still wears the same brand of aftershave.

He smells so good. How is she going to resist him?

'Are you coming?' Roch asks as he takes her hand and starts to walk.

As they go hand in hand Fanny tries not to look at his hairy chest and does her best not to smell his aftershave.

Roch enjoys showing her Toronto. It is not her favourite city, but Fanny is quite impressed by it. She imagines them back in time—two lovers very much in love trying to make the most of their little time together.

Roch is happy. This reminds him of the first time he brought her to his family's cottage. She had never seen something so beautiful and so rich. That day they went for a boat ride. She sat at the back of the boat, laughing, her long hair like *Bardot* flying in her face. She looked so carefree and happy.

He always wondered why he went out with her. She never wore make-up, was never dressed like the other girls, because she could not afford it. Her hair was always long, straight, and loose. She had nothing special, though she did have nice legs.

With plenty of money and a reputation for being the town playboy, Roch was always going out with pretty girls. He liked then well-dressed, with make-up and nice hairdos. So what was he doing with Fanny, that year? Fanny fascinated him, she reminded him of a child—everything seemed like magic to her.

That day he had stopped the boat and gotten closer to her. He had taken her in his arms and kissed her for the first time. He had then caressed her neck, passed his hand through her hair and, slowly, had undone the buttons of her blouse. He wanted her!

Fanny was very shy and was embarrassed by his actions. She got up, took out her comb, and started to fix her hair.

Roch did not insist and went back to start the boat. They

didn't say another word for the rest of the trip.

Coming back to the present Roch looked at Fanny. How she looked impressed! You could tell that she had not travelled much.

At that moment the wind swept through Fanny's curly hair.

How Roch wished he could take her into his arms and kiss her, but at that very moment the sun chose to shine on Fanny's wedding band. Roch contemplated it for a long time and taking Fanny's hand finally said, 'Come, there's still a lot of things I want to show you.'

CHAPTER III

'You know that the Saturday banquet is formal, which means black tie and full dress.'

'Oh!'said Fanny.

Tears came to her eyes as she told herself, 'It's always the same; I won't fit in— once again.'

Fanny cannot help but think of the time she was a teenager. How cruel some of the girls at school were with her. They always laughed at her hand-me-down clothes.

She remembered one night especially, when she was at the movie theatre with Roch. While he went to get some snacks, three of his old girlfriends came by to speak to her.

'Well, look who's here—the poor girl that Roch picked up,' said Sue.

'Poor Roch, he must be so ashamed to be seen with her. Look how she is dressed!' remarked Louise.

'Bet it won't take long before he dumps her. As soon as she gives in, Roch will win the bet and we will see him more again,' replied Rita.

When they saw Roch coming back, they hurried up to their seats.

Holding back her tears Fanny takes the chocolate bar and the orange pop that Roch gives her.

Roch smiles at her and she smiles back. Good, the movie is starting!

Fanny looks at the yellow dress that her mother has made for her to wear on Sundays and on special occasions. Then she looks at Roch. He is always elegantly dressed. No wonder he gets all the women he wants. Fanny is mad at him. How could he! She wants to scream at him and leave, but a movie theatre is not the place to make a scene.

It's a good movie, Roch is happy to have brought Fanny. He knows how much she likes sad stories. Smiling he looks at her, she is crying. He puts his arm around her and kisses her tears.

'Sorry,' she apologizes, 'sad movies always make me cry.'

Roch holds her tight. Sue, Louise and Rita watch from a distance. For a moment their eyes meet Fanny's. Fanny smiles back at them and puts her head on Roch's shoulders.

Did he really make a bet? Is he staying with me only until I go to bed with him? So you think you're so smart, she thought, as she looked at the three girls. You want Roch? Well, you will have to wait a long time. You just gave me the secret to keep Roch. I am not pretty or rich, my virginity is the only thing that I have. Well, if Roch wants to sleep with me, he will have to marry me first.

Suddenly Roch's voice brings her back to the present.

'Is everything ok?'

They are in a theatre in Toronto, waiting for a play to start.

'I am sure you will like it, *Les Misérables* by Hugo.'

'Did you ever finish that novel or were you content with

reading only my notes that I lent you at school?'

'Never! I'm no fan of literature, I'm not a fanatic like you,' he answered laughing.

'Fanatic! Dare to say that my notes didn't come in handy.'

The curtain opens, Roch and Fanny stop talking.

For a moment Fanny is so involved in the play that she forgets everything.

Suddenly she looks at her dress. What a coincidence, her dress is yellow. She smiles and looks at Roch. Always elegant! The cruel words that Sue, Louise and Rita had said to her many years ago come back to her mind suddenly.

While on the stage poor Fantine sells everything she has in order to send more money for her little daughter's keep, Fanny can no longer hold her tears. At that moment Roch looks at her. He wipes the tears off her cheek with his fingers and then he takes her in his arms. In unison, they say, 'Sad movies always make me cry.'

Two days have passed since they went to the theatre. Fanny is sitting on a chair in her room, her head tipped backwards, her feet up. She has her arms wrapped around them and she is looking at the big box on her bed.

She hardly slept because the night before they went to a nightclub where the orchestra played old songs. They had fun joking and dancing. That last waltz, pressed up close against each other, their bodies shivering with desire—ah! if only the dance could have lasted forever!

Back at the hotel Roch asked her what her plans were for the next day.

'My plan is to go to bed early. This week was wonderful, but I should rest. I'm very tired. I'll have a long day on the bus going back home.'

'I too plan to go to bed early. I was thinking, if I rented a movie, would you be interested to join me in my room after the banquet?'

Fanny gets up early. It is her last day in Toronto. Although she looks forward to seeing her family, yet she is sad.

Knock! Knock!

CHAPTER IV

Roch is lying on his bed. There is a knock. He gets up, opens the door. It is Fanny—standing there looking lovely.

He looks at her. The dress he bought suits her beautifully. He signals her to come in.

Fanny walks slowly. She is not at ease. The dress he chose for her is very low cut.

When Fanny had opened the big box brought to her by the room service attendant, she had felt for a while as if she was Cinderella. Her fairy godmother had not forgotten her. In the big box, there was a long, sexy, blue silk dress with this message:

I hope you like it!

She had a long look at herself in the mirror. The dress was beautiful! She *knew then* that she had to go to his room after the banquet.

Roch was expecting her. On the nightstand there is an orange pop and a box of chocolates.

They smile at each other. She is so beautiful! Roch would like to hold her tight and kiss her and get her out of that nice, sexy, blue silk dress. 'She is so fragile, she looks like a teenager on her first date,' he says to himself.

Roch hands her a glass of orange soda.

'Come sit down,' he says as he fluffs the pillows.

Fanny takes her shoes off and sits on the other side of the bed at a distance from Roch. He smells so good. She senses that she should not have come.

They talk about the week that has gone by—the seminar, the hotel service, and *Les Miserables*. We sure look like two birds perched on a branch gabbing loudly, thinks Roch. How can I tell her that I want her without scaring her away?

'Well, let's watch the film.' Roch gets up and puts the movie on. They sit in silence.

Fanny is very tired and falls asleep. Roch looks at her and smiles. She is cold. As she shivers and curls into a foetal position, he takes her into his arms.

Ah! it is so cosy! Fanny thinks she is in Emile's arms. She gets closer to Roch and puts her leg on top of him. Gently, Roch caresses her leg, takes a peek at her breasts. Fanny gets closer to him and aims for his lips. Ah! what a feeling! Emile and I should do this more often.

Suddenly, she remembers that she is with Roch. Quickly, she sits up and says, 'I'm really tired. I should go.'

'No, stay. This is nice. Please, stay.'

Yes, this *is* very nice. Yes, let's stay for a while, she convinces herself as she settles back into his arms. He kisses the top of her hair and holding each other tightly they keep on watching the movie.

But as the movie gets very romantic, Roch starts kissing Fanny passionately. She shivers when he caresses her leg and kisses her breasts. Yes, she says to herself, take me, I want you so much!

'Spend the night with me,' he murmurs in her ear as he tenderly positions himself on top of her.

The world has stopped for Fanny. Roch smells so good, the hair on his chest is so smooth, it's so nice to be in his arm. Everything is perfect!

'Stop,' she suddenly shouts, 'please stop! This is not right!' She pushes him off and manages to get out of the bed.

She tries to fix her dress, her breasts half exposed.

'How much did you bet that you would sleep with me?' she yells at him.

Surprised Roch looks at her; he doesn't understand.

'What are you talking about?'

'I'm talking about the bet you made with your friends.'

'I don't understand, what bet?'

Roch has only one thing in mind—to have her back in his arms.

Fanny looks him up. 'Didn't you bet you'd get me to make love to you before you'd dump me.'

'I don't remember ever saying that.'

'Well, to refresh your memory, why not ask your old girlfriends—Sue, Louise and Rita?'

'Ah, you're talking about twenty years ago. Bah, those girls were jealous of you. They only went out with me for my money.'

Grabbing her by the arms, he adds, 'Listen, whatever they told you, I certainly would never have bet something like that.'

Then, tenderly, he whispers, 'Come back in my arms.

Spend the night with me.'

Fanny finds it hard to resist. The hair on his chest is so soft, he smells so good. NO! She can't; she has to be strong.

'Let go of me! You're hurting me.'

Roch lets her go. Fanny starts to pace and asks him, 'Why were you going out with me, then?—And why am I here anyway? Do you love me?'

Yes, why? he asks himself. Do I love her?

Roch doesn't know what to say. The silence is killing Fanny. She cannot take it anymore, she is very angry. She turns to face him, tears streaming from her eyes.

'What is all this?—visiting Toronto, the dancing, the play, and that beautiful, sexy, blue silk dress? Are you trying to relive the past? The handsome, rich boy feels retrospectively sorry for the poor, ugly girl, so he buys her some nice gifts? What game are you playing?'

Choked with emotion Fanny has trouble speaking. She is so beautiful, so fragile standing defenceless against her sobs. Roch would like to take her in his arms, but he knows it is too late.

'Do you remember your last words to me?' she cries. '"My parents don't want me to go out with you anymore. They are sending me to Toronto to study . Listen, Fanny, I can't do anything now, but wait for me; I'll come back to you." What a great promise! It didn't take long that everybody was talking about the beautiful, rich girl you were about to marry. The hardest part was that you didn't even have the courage to tell me. Not even a letter—nothing! That night, I cried so much that I couldn't work. Emile Millaire was working at the same restaurant and he covered for me. If not for him, I would have lost my job. He helped me get over you. He's a very nice guy.'

She looks right into Roch's eyes and insists, 'What do you want from me? Make love once—and then what? A little fling and that's it! Is it worth it?'

Roch listens without uttering a word.

Fanny wipes her tears and pulls up her dress while she keeps on talking, 'No, you're not the only one who's playing a game. I'm no better than you. I'm also playing that game. What am I doing here? I'm a happily married woman, with children. What do I want? An adventure? Who doesn't dream of one? A nice love story! Our story would've finished wonderfully if you'd married me! I would have worked. I would have done anything in order for you to finish university! At least, we would have been together; our life would have been like a children's storybook—"*and they lived happily ever after and had lots of children.*»'

Fanny starts laughing.

'You know,' she tells him, 'I am happy that we met again. All these years, you've been a shadow on my marriage. While talking to you, I suddenly realised how lucky I am. My husband may not be Prince Charming, but our love is solid. Come to think of it, he's better that me—I was about to lose all we have for one night of sex? I must be crazy!'

Fanny leaves for the bathroom. She looks at herself in the mirror; her make-up is running down her face. She grabs a towel.

She comes back into the room, puts her shoes on. Slowly,

very very slowly, she lets the long ... sexy, blue, silk dress ... fall to the floor.

'Take a good look at my body!' she says, as she wraps the towel around herself.

For the last time, she looks at Roch—his gray temples, his hair on his chest, his body that smells so good, and his beautiful, green eyes. It's over, it's really over!

Theirs eyes meet one last time. Shaking, Fanny leaves the room.

Roch, still sitting on the bed, stares at the sexy, blue, silk dress on the floor. He gets up, picks up the dress, and utters, 'I will marry the girl who fits in this dress!'

THE END

The Wanderer
of New Perry

To my 'Wild Stallion'
My muse
2003-2007

Thank you, Richard, my little brother!

You are my muse!

You are my muse!
My sunshine!
My inspiration!

I see you
And I think
Of tender thoughts!

"I anticipate the day you will take me in your arms!
I imagine the taste of your lips
I look forward to the day
When I will explore every inch of your body
I want you so much!"

You are my muse!
My sunshine!
My inspiration!

Without you!
I am nothing!
Without you!
I cannot create!

You are my muse!
My sunshine!
My inspiration!

FC

The wind was very strong that night. The rain was falling very hard. The trees were bending and the streetlights looked as if they were dancing.

It was dark. You couldn't see—those who didn't have to go out stayed in where it was warm.

Through the widow of an apartment we see a woman.

She is very tired. She has worked very late that night. When she got home, she sat for a minute.

After changing her work clothes for a pair of jeans and a blouse she went to the kitchen to prepare her supper.

Suddenly, she stopped what she was doing and listened. It sounded like somebody was screaming!

She listened again; she shut the stove off, went to the window, and looked out.

It was too dark to see anything, the wind and the rain were too strong.

She looked at the clock. '8 o'clock, who would be outside in weather like this?'

Something was wrong, she was scared. She did not have a choice, she would have to check it out.

She put her coat on and wrapped a scarf around her head, took her umbrella and went outside.

She could not see, but she heard it again—she guided herself by following the screams.

She saw three men hitting someone.

She told them to stop, but they ignored her.

So she took her umbrella and started hitting them. They left without any further hesitation.

The victim was not making any sounds. With baited breath, the woman bent to see if he was dead or alive.

The man started to move. He put his hand on his head.

The woman asked him, 'Are you OK? May I help you?'

He did not answer; he was still holding his head.

She bent down to be at his level.

Quickly, the man put his hand over his right pocket; he did not want her to steal what he had in there. It was very precious to him and he would defend it with his life.

'Are you able to get up?' she asked, as she grabbed his arm to help him.

She had forgotten about the darkness, the rain and the wind—her main concern was that man.

Once he stood up, she told him, 'Come with me, I live nearby. I want to see how badly you're hurt.'

'I'm able to take care of myself,' he replied, taking his arm from the woman's hand.

He started to walk.

When the woman saw that he was staggering, she grasped his hand and brought him to her apartment.

* * * * *

She sat him in a chair and started to examine him.

She could not tell his age exactly. He was somewhere between 50 or 60 years old. He had gray hair and a gray beard. He was wearing a black hat, a blue shirt, blue jeans, brown shoes, and a black coat with the name "Antoine" embroidered on it. He was very tall—5' 9" maybe?—in good shape for his age, no beer belly. He was kind of good-looking, except that his face had pockmarks. When their eyes met, she found them beautiful, but she could not tell what color they were.

She smiled at him. He returned her smile and said, 'May I go now?'

He put his hand on his treasure.

She stopped daydreaming and replied, 'Let's me see your head.'

She took his head in her hands and examined it.

The man took a deep breath, his nostrils filling with the woman's fragrance.

She smelled good. She smelled like roses. It had been a long time since he had smelt something so good! It reminded him of the good old days.

He had known lots of women, but he did not remember them smelling so good.

For a moment he wanted to hold her tight, to nuzzle his nose in between her breasts. How funny it was that he had not felt that need for a long, long time. Would he still be able to use it? Could he still have a hard-on?

Before he had time to react, the woman had already gone

and come back. She washed his wound with alcohol and a cotton ball and put a bandage on it.

He smiled at her again and advised her that it was time for him to leave.

'You should see a doctor. What about your family? Let me call them.'

The man looked at her and declared, 'I feel good. I want to go.'

'I was about to have supper, why don't you join me?'

Again he put his hand in his pocket, he was so thirsty. He was very, very, thirsty!

Before he had time to respond, she took his hand and brought him to the table.

Angry, the man kicked the chair. Surprised by his action the woman said to herself, 'He looks like a wild stallion. He is badly in need to be tame!'

She insisted, 'You cannot GO, not in this condition!'

'What condition?'

'You've just been attacked. You CANNOT leave NOW!'

The look he gave her left her frozen inside, but she did not have time for such nonsense.

She picked the chair up and ordered him to sit!

He sat, but he was not very happy about it. Would that woman ever leave him alone? He just wanted to go! He was very thirsty—very, very thirsty.

She took a plate, filled it with food, and passed it to him, then served herself. She was hungry, so she started to eat.

The man sat there for a long time looking at her. He was not happy. He just wanted to go. But after a while, he decided that it was best to eat. They did not speak. At the end of the supper she saw that he seemed more content.

From time to time he put his hand in his pocket. He was thirsty, even the coffee that she poured him did not help to quench his thirst!

'I made a chocolate cake, would you like a piece?'

She was up before he had time to answer.

When she came back, he was gone.

* * * * *

She put the two pieces of cake on the table and went to the window.

She could not see him.

Then she saw something on the couch. She went to see what it was. It was him!

The man was lying down, already asleep. She took off his hat, she undid his coat, took off his shoes. As she was covering him with a blanket she noticed that he was holding a little flask of whisky. She took it away from him and he grunted.

She stood there looking at him. Who was he? She needed to know!

She removed his wallet, opened it. and read "Antoine

Dubeau." Well at least he had a name—"Antoine Dubeau, 467 Bird Street."

So he does not live in the street. Thus he is not a beggar or a tramp.

She put the wallet back, the man did not react. He was too drunk.

She went to her room, grabbed her two pillows, and put them under his head. She knew that it was best for people to sleep half-sitting up when they were drunk.

She ate the two pieces of cake. She washed the dishes and, after waiting in vain for him to wake up, she finally went to bed.

It was hard to sleep without a pillow, and having a stranger in the house kept her awake for a long time. But she was tired and, finally, she fell asleep.

* * * * *

The next morning, she went to check on him, only to find him gone. He had left without saying "Thank you!"

The woman sat down to think about it all.

Who was that stranger who had come to disrupt her life? That tall and handsome stranger, built like a God, graceful and elegant like a stallion, who had such beautiful eyes!

But she didn't have time to think about it any further, she had to get ready for work.

She put her dirty clothes in the hamper and then jumped into the shower. After she was finished, she cleaned the bathroom. As she was walking to her room, she saw her reflection in the mirror.

She let her towel fall and took a good look at herself.

Her breasts were still in a good firm shape, although she had breastfed her children. She touched her belly. She let her fingers dance on her stretch marks and said, 'What nice memories!'

Was she still pretty? She had big eyes, big ears, a big nose, and an aging face. No, she was not pretty!

Was she still appealing to men?

Would a man want her?

'Flavie Croissant, are you being flirtatious?' she said laughing at herself.

Why was she thinking about that now?

She was free, free like a bird! Why now?

Flavie Croissant was 54 years old, had two children, and after many years of marriage left her husband. An affair had left her bitter and she had decided to cross men out of her life.

She did not need them, she could make it on her own. Cleaning houses in the mornings and working three evenings a week as a dishwasher in a restaurant had helped her make ends meet.

This morning was supposed to be like any other morning, except today, she could not stop thinking of the tramp with the beautiful eyes!

* * * * *

'I will not be finished in time!' Flavie exclaimed. 'Why did Madame Dubois have to ask me to clean her house on a Monday? I won't have time to eat again before I go to my other job!'

Madame Dubois might be her best client, but she was very demanding and she often found things for her to do at the last minute!

Madame Dubois liked to talk and often Flavie would miss her bus and have to wait for the next one.

'Rich people really don't understand those of us who have to work so hard to make a living or else they have no sense at all of how precious our time is!'

Flavie ran home as soon as the bus came to a stop. She took off her clothes, threw them on her bed, and jumped into her uniform.

She threw some fruits into her lunch bag. Yes, the restaurant did give her a discount on her meals, but she tried not to eat greasy foods. It is so hard to keep your weight down when you are 54.

She ran to the restaurant, which was located only three streets from her apartment. She pushed the door open.

The boss shouted, 'Late again!'

She looked at him and chose not to say anything. What could she say, really?

Her apron on, she plunged her hands into the dish water.

Euclide, the cook, busy preparing meals, asked her how she was doing.

Josiane, the waitress, burst in and told Euclide and Flavie, 'It's going very well. They're really tipping tonight. That's good!'

Flavie was finally on her break. She sat down to drink a cup of coffee and eat her fruit. Her feet up, she listened to the customers talking to one another.

Always the same people, always the same faces, always the same problems! She has heard their problems so many times that she could recite them!

She started thinking of him, the wanderer with those beautiful eyes. Oh! how she wished Yvette was there. She knew everybody, so surely she would know about Antoine Dubeau.

Who was that man who had disrupted her life so much?

* * * * *

Friday night and it was still raining. When would the rain stop? Flavie was very tired. She had spent the morning washing walls and the evenings washing dishes at the restaurant, so she walked slowly.

She could not wait to get home and jump into a hot bath. Ah! to be home! It would be so nice to be able to sleep in on her day off tomorrow.

When she walked by the liquor store she slowed down. Her heart was beating very hard. What if he was inside? She would see him again. Yes, she wanted to see him again!

Some people came out, but none of them were him. Just because he bought himself a whisky one night does not mean that he drinks often.

'Flavie, what is the matter with you?' she told herself. 'You can't sleep. You can't eat. Is it because you are too exhausted? Can you tell me why you were walking on his street the other night? I understand you walking by the liquor store—it's close to home, but his street isn't. You'd better be careful, if you get too tired, you may lose your job!—Flavie, that wanderer sure is making you *wako* and you don't even know him. Before, you were free and happy, and now—are you going to lose it for a man that you don't even know?'

'He is not a wanderer, he has a house! And that flask of whisky that he kept hidden in his pocket? What do you think that meant? Please forget about him, you are not going to see him again!'

'Look, last week you were crying when you were listening to music and you did not know why. Are you going to ruin your life for a stranger?—But he has such beautiful eyes! Why did he have to come and disturb my tranquil life?'

* * * * *

Flavie could hear her, she recognised her voice. That laugh—only she had a laugh like that. The clients are restless, they are loud. Flavie cannot wait to speak to her about her tramp with the beautiful eyes.

But Yvette (yes, it is her) is too busy to stop for a break. She only has time to smile at Flavie.

Yvette works fast. She has been working in that same restaurant ever since she was fourteen and she knows her customers. She knows everybody—their stories, their life—and she never forgets anything. That is why people come—because she provides them with a sympathetic ear.

'Pierre, how is your back?'

'I'm going to the chiropractor three times a month; it's getting there. I feel good!'

'Mariette, your operation, is it soon?'

'No, they changed the date again!'

'He's a quack, go see another one!'

'Louis and Marie-Jeanne are grandparents—it's a boy. '

'Finally! They have waited so long for that grandchild! '

'Mario, would you like another piece of cake? '

'Sure, Yvette, why not? '

And that is the way it goes all day. Yvette is so busy, you could believe that the restaurant was hers!

'Yvette, I prepared a sandwich and a bowl of soup for you. Come and sit down. '

'Thanks, Euclide, you take such good care of me. '

And while Yvette sits and eats, she talks to Euclide and Josiane.

Flavie is washing the dishes. She would like to speak to Yvette as well, but she is too busy chatting. She does not have time for Flavie!

When her break is over, Yvette sidles up to Flavie.

'Are you OK, Flavie? You are not saying much.'

'I'm OK!'

Flavie looks at Euclide. He is back to work and Josiane is getting ready to serve a customer. She takes a deep breath and asks, 'Yvette, do you know Antoine Dubeau?'

'He's a big tramp and an old drunk. He's not worth thinking about. If he was the only man on earth, I would tell you not to get close to him. Better to stay single than be married to that man!'

Yvette goes back to work and Flavie to washing dishes. She can't help but think about Antoine Dubeau. How nice would it be if she were the only woman on earth and he the only man? 'Our children would have such beautiful eyes!'

*　*　*　*　*

'Why do you insist so much on knowing about him?'

Flavie tells Yvette how she met Antoine Dubeau and saved his life.

'So, you saved his life—what else to you want? '

'I'm just curious to know who he is. I cannot believe that there is not one nice thing that you can say about him. Everybody has a good side and a bad side.'

'Well not him! He's always mad. And if you bother him, he will kick whatever is in his way!'

With that, Yvette returns to take care of her customers.

Yvette looks at Flavie. She is still musing about her tramp. Yvette thinks to herself, 'Poor Flavie. She doesn't have any life, so she attaches herself to a man who is worthless. We have to find her a companion soon!"

* * * * *

Flavie is singing while she cleans the living room of one of her clients. She often sings when she is alone.

She is happier today. As she cleans, she can't help but think of him.

'I wonder what he does. What kind of man is he? Does he work? Is he married? Does he have kids? I wish Yvette would tell me all that she knows about him.'

Flavie scrubs, scrubs, and scrubs. A blue jay comes and sits on the window sill.

She looks at him and finds him so beautiful.

She talks to him, 'Pretty bird, do you know a certain tramp with beautiful eyes? If you know him, could you go and tell him that I would like to see him again? I wish I had wings. I would fly—first, to the liquor store and then to his house. I would be able to follow him wherever he went. Maybe then would I find out the color of his eyes!'

'Beautiful bird, how lucky you are to be able to fly wherever you want! As for me, I am just a poor woman who waits—yes, waits—for what?—for—love?—friendship?—a life?"

'Come on, Flavie, go back to work! If your client was to come and see you like this, what would you tell her?'

'I would tell her'—laughing at the thought of it— 'I would tell her that I want to be a bird, so I can fly away, very far away from here to a ... special street ...'

* * * * *

Yvette has decided to tell Flavie everything she knows about Antoine Dubeau. As they sip their coffee Flavie listens carefully.

After what seems like an eternity Yvette starts. 'Antoine and I come from the same hometown. We went to school together. He is younger that me ... I think. It's hard to know because of his gray hair.'

'But his hair is so nice. It reminds me of cotton!'

Yvette gives Flavie a dirty look. But then, this *is* Flavie, so she should not be surprised by the way she expresses herself!

Yvette takes another sip of her coffee and then continues, 'He never knew his father, who died when he was a baby. His mother remarried and had four more children with her new husband—two boys and two girls. His step-father was very strict with Antoine. He used to make him work really hard. Antoine left home when he was old enough to support himself. He had to work hard to make it on his own. But then, he had always worked hard. Sometimes, he had two jobs—one during the day and one in the evenings. He's been drinking for as long as I've known him.'

'He drank, even when he was young?' questioned Flavie.

'Yes, even at school. I remember that he was always sucking on candies so we could not smell his breath, but we were not stupid!'

'Why do you call him a tramp, if he works all the time?'

'I don't know! Maybe because he always looks dirty and he stinks! And he also gets very mad and does not like it when people talk to him. What a big difference though when he is drunk! Then, he is so nice!'

'Oh yeah?'

'He used to come here for his coffee, but he likes to be alone so he stopped coming here. He spends his summers camping. He likes to be in the great outdoors.'

'Is he married? Does he have any children?'

'He was married more than once. Children? I know that he has some, but how many I don't know. You know, I have not seen him much since he left school!'

'How come he was married more that once?'

'How do I know! Didn't I tell you that he was a drunk and that he gets mad very easily? Who wants to be married to a drunk?'

'Where does he work?'

'At the Sunset—he's their maintenance man. He also does some work on the side. That man is a jack-of-all-trade. He can do whatever you ask. But his Saturday nights he spends them at The Wizard.'

'The Wizard? What is that?'

'It's a bar. He drinks, you know ...'

* * * * *

Euclide is looking at Flavie. He wants to speak to her but he does not know how. He is very shy, does not say much. He is a hard worker who never thinks twice about giving someone a hand.

From the very first Flavie knew that she could count on Euclide. He was a huge man and that scared some people at first. But, in no time at all, they would notice that he was a sweetheart. He was always putting others first, making sure they took the time to eat; so he always had a sandwich, a cup of soup, some crackers, whatever, ready for them.

Even though he does not say anything bad about the others, he still likes good gossip. That is why he likes working in the restaurant. He may be stuck at the back in the kitchen, but he always knows what is going on out front because if it is not Yvette that tells him, it is Josiane—she likes nothing better than to repeat what she hears.

Josiane needed to know other people's business so badly, it was almost like a disease. She liked to know everything and she liked nothing better than to repeat it. At first Flavie did not trust her. Now, she was used to her ... though not to the point of telling her any of her secrets.

When Josiane left the kitchen, Euclide came up to Flavie and slowly said, 'Flavie, Yvette tells me you're interested in Antoine Dubeau, is it true? Trust me—you want to stay away from him.'

'Why?'

'The reason he does not come to the café any more is because the boss has forbidden him from coming back!'

'But why?'

'He is always in a bad mood. You can't talk to him when he is angry!'

'Who are you talking about, Euclide?' tossed Josiane, who

had just come back into the kitchen.

'Antoine Dubeau!'

'Is that the drunk that used to come here before?'

'Yes!'

'I always talked to him when he came here and then, one day, he told me to shut up—that he had had enough of my gossip. Gossip! Me? I don't gossip!'

And Josiane returned to serve her customers.

Euclide started to laugh, Flavie started to laugh also. They both laughed until tears came to their eyes.

* * * * *

'The Sunset ... That's where I am!' murmured Flavie. 'That's where he works—at a nursing home!'

Flavie holds a brochure that explains how this nursing home is a pleasant place to live. She notices a paragraph: *At Sunset, we are always looking for volunteers! If you care about older people, this is where we could use your help!*

'Hey! that's not bad, it looks like a nice place. Volunteer work ... why not? ... Antoine Dubeau works there!'

'Don't even think about it!' Flavie told herself on second thought. 'You hardly have time for your two jobs as it is ... you want to start doing volunteer work too?'

'Antoine Dubeau works there! So what! I could finally see him!'

'And what is your point? I walk and walk in front of the liquor store and I don't see him! And then, I walk in front of his house and I don't see him! I could go to The Wizard, but I don't drink and I'm scared to go there alone! I don't know what else to do!'

'Yes, I know ... I'm crazy. I have to see him! He is so handsome and he has such beautiful eyes!'

All day, Flavie debates whether she should go or forget about it all.

'I'll think about it tomorrow!' she tells herself, as she gets into her bed.

* * * * *

Flavie is at The Sunset. She has decided that volunteering to work with senior citizens could be rewarding.

While she is waiting to be called for her appointment she scans the premises. There are lots of people.

'How crazy are you! You have two jobs, you hardly have any time for yourself, and now you are signing up to do volunteer work! How long are you going to lie to yourself? So you say that the reason you wanted to work with the seniors is because you never knew your grandparents! Why are you looking just like you are searching for someone?'

'He works here, Yvette told me so!'

A woman comes and says, 'You are the new volunteer? Then you will be working with me. Come, I'll show you around.'

Flavie follows the lady. She meets lots of people. As they are walking, the supervisor introduces her to the staff, to the senior citizens, everybody that they come across.

But ... Flavie does not see Antoine Dubeau. Does he really work here?

She writes down in her notebook what is expected of her, but she does not see Antoine Dubeau.

So she dares to ask, 'What do you do if something breaks?'

* * * * *

Flavie has been at The Sunset two weeks now and she still has not seen Antoine!

Since she does not see him at the Sunset, she continues to walk by his house and the liquor store.

As hard as she tries, she still does not run into him! There are lots of people on the street, but she is apprehensive that she will not see him again!

* * * * *

Working at the Sunset is very rewarding because the old people have so much to offer. They enjoy telling her about their life.

While Flavie listens, she makes so that they talk about Antoine.

They also tell her that Antoine likes to go camping. When he is not working he leaves New Perry. He likes nature and there is no better place than the country to get fresh air.

'Where is he now?' she dares ask one day.

'He's gone hunting.'

'Oh yeah! Will he be gone long?'

* * * * *

One day at Madame Dubois', she sees Antoine!

He is busy in her garage. Up on a ladder he is working laboriously.

Flavie cannot believe it! 'It's him, I am quite sure. Yes, it *is* him!'

For a moment their eyes meet. 'Did he recognize me?'

She cannot stop looking at him!

But she must be careful. Madame Dubois is not too far away, she might see her.

She would like to question Madame Dubois, but she can't. Madame Dubois might wonder why she is interested in Antoine.

'Flavie, did you notice that we are redoing our garage? We will be putting in a swimming pool. Do you see that man? He is the best guy to repair, construct, or invent anything. There is nothing that he can't do. It's too bad that he drinks and that he loses his temper so easily!'

* * * * *

The next day, Antoine is at The Sunset. He is looking at her. She thinks he has recognized her.

Flavie says, 'Hello! How are you?'

'Don't talk to me.'

'Do you know who I am?'

'I told you not to talk to me!'

'Why? Is something wrong?'

'Would you shut up!'

'You do remember me, don't you?'

'How many times do I have to tell you to be quiet?'

'Do you remember the night of that big storm? Three men were attacking you and I came to your rescue!'

'Shut up means, keep your mouth shut!'

Antoine throws the broom he was holding and leaves.

Flavie looks at him go and says, 'What a strange man! He is savage and very wild!'

* * * * *

The next day when Flavie has to pass by him, she walks slowly. She does not want to make him angry!

But what a surprise, Antoine looks at her and he smiles. Flavie smiles back.

So she stops walking and asks, 'Do I have permission to ... talk to you, today?'

'Of course,' he responds with a big smile on his face.

'How do we know when we ... are able to ... talk to you?'

'Just ask, and I will tell you!'

'If you don't, then what?'

'You don't talk to me!'

'Why?'

'Because I'm not in the mood to talk!'

'What if I don't care whether you are or not in the mood?'

'I don't like it when people talk to me when I don't feel like it!'

Flavie thinks for a moment and then replies, 'You remind me of a volcano.'

'Why is that?'

'We know that it's there, but we never know when it's going to erupt!'

'You just have to leave me alone when I'm not in the mood!' retorts Antoine. Obviously he is getting impatient!

Flavie got the message. She looked at him and added, 'Then you are such a big baby!'

Exasperated, Antoine shrugs his shoulders and leaves the room.

*   *   *   *   *

Seeing that Antoine is in a bad mood Flavie stays away from him. It is no use getting yelled at for nothing.

And then, one day, he smiles at her. She smiles back, he

has such a lovely smile!

He works not too far from where she is. From time to time Flavie glances at him. He also looks at her, and they smile.

*   *   *   *   *

Flavie is happy. She likes her volunteer work at The Sunset. It helps that Antoine works there also.

Sometimes he lets her speak to him, but he does not seem to recall that night of the big storm. If he remembers that she is the one ... who saved him ... he does not talk about it! It would be nice if he would thank her for that. But he does not!

Flavie is allowed to talk to him as long as she does not ask personal questions. He is not interested in other people's problems—especially not those of Flavie's private life.

Some days, it is nice to speak with Antoine and then there are other days when it is better to keep your mouth shut. When Antoine is angry, you know by his eyes—they are bigger. That is when Flavie stays distant from him!

Antoine is a bit strange. There are days he neither looks at Flavie nor speaks to her. Others times, he will look at her and even smile. It is as though Flavie's existence depended on his mood.

Flavie has learned to accept his moodiness, but she finds his bad days so long. She wants nothing more than to talk to him!

One day when she was about to disclose something personal to him, he told her flat that he had enough with his own problems, he had no intention of burdening himself with other people's problems.

Another day, when he was in a fury, he threw at her, 'I have work to do. I don't have time for gossip.'

'I'm not gossiping,' yelled Flavie. 'I'm talking to you!'

＊　＊　＊　＊　＊

Flavie has studied Antoine's every move. She knows where he will be at a certain time of the day and at what specific moment.

Naturally she organises her time to be at the same place at the very same hour he will be working—without, of course, letting her work suffer.

Flavie goes up a different flight of stairs than she is supposed to, just for the chance to meet him. When she learns that Antoine is on his break at eleven o'clock, she fixes her break to match his.

She must see him! She will do anything to see him!

＊　＊　＊　＊　＊

Flavie organizes her life around her two jobs and her volunteer work. The three fulfill her needs.

Her work in private houses give her tranquility. Flavie likes to dream and, since she is alone most of the time in the house, she is free to dream as much as she likes! Because she lives alone, her work as a dishwasher at the restaurant helps her meet people and socialize. There is also Euclide, Josiane and, of course, Yvette. She considers her a true friend and views her as a sister.

One day Yvette, asks her, 'So your tramp, have you finally seen him?'

Flavie does not answer. She prefers not to let anybody know that her volunteer work gives her the chance to see Antoine Dubeau, the wanderer with beautiful eyes!—those beautiful eyes which she cannot restrain herself from ...

Every time she can, she looks at him. She thinks he is so attractive! When she looks at him, she knows that Antoine is aware of it—even though he does not say anything! Does that bother him? Does he like it? He is so good looking!

When Flavie sees that it is all right to talk to him, she asks him many questions. She has noticed that he is very intelligent and that he knows lots of stuff. As she starts to know him better, she finds that he has many qualities.

He likes the rain, the wind, the snow—routine is not a bore for him! She finds him nice, even helpful, with other people, always ready to give a hand. No task is too big or too hard to handle!

Flavie notices that he never says anything inconsiderate about anybody. He does not swear. At times he is gallant enough to open the door for her. Flavie likes a man who is not afraid to show his masculinity.

Nothing scares him! Nothing at all! NOTHING—except Flavie!

He does not say much, does not talk for nothing! Sometimes he will joke with others—but never with Flavie.

There are times when Flavie knows that her presence pesters him. She just has to pronounce his name and his eyes show her that he wishes she would disappear. In those moments she does not dare to bother him. Sadly, she leaves. Is that a sign that he does not love her?

But her, she DOES LOVE HIM!

She loves to be in his company. She could spend hours looking at him. As soon as he appears, she goes to him. Any chance she gets, she finds something to talk to him about.

He is like a magnet! It is as if her body did not have any strength to stay away from him.

Flavie likes Antoine's magnificent hands, his great body, his gorgeous butt, his enchanting eyes, and she wonders what he would look like naked.

'How do you tame a man that has everything? Beauty ... intelligence ... and grace!'

* * * * *

Flavie and Antoine have been working together for quite a while now. One day Antoine asks her, 'Do you like camping?'

'If I sleep in a motel room!'

'I see!'

Two days later, Flavie questions Antoine, 'Why did you ask me if I like camping?'

'It was just to make conversation!'

'I don't mind camping if I sleep in a bed. I don't like to sleep on the ground, it's hard on the back and, when it rains, you get wet. I hate the rain! It makes me sad!!!'

'I have a camper, so we don't have to sleep on the ground! I go camping every weekend from May to September—sometimes in winter too. As soon as I finish work, I run away. I suffocate in town! I spend my summers camping and autumns hunting.'

'Oh! I see! I like nature, I was raised on a farm. But when you asked me that ... I don't really know you! I ... I don't go to bed with men I don't know. And I am not that easy! You have to know that I was a virgin when I got married and I was married for a long time.'

'Oh, no, no! I was not thinking about that! I was just talking, you know, to make conversation. I was just curious to know if you liked camping. And, besides, there are two beds in my camper.'

And to justify himself Antoine adds, 'I adore camping, I've been doing it since I was that high—' and Antoine gestures with his hands to show her how tall he was when he started camping.

They don't say any more, but Antoine has to admit to himself that Flavie is in love with him. She always seems to find herself in the same rooms he is in. Antoine likes to be alone.

* * * * *

'Antoine, I have found room for your boxes. Come and see!'

'No, I don't have time!'

'Come on, it's only going to take a minute!'

'Leave me alone!'

'Come on, it will only be a minute!'

'No, go away!'

Flavie stands there waiting for him, hoping he will change his mind, but Antoine keeps on working, ignoring her.

'Well, then!' she sighs as she decides to leave!

* * * * *

'Antoine, I must tell you something.'

'I don't care to hear it!'

'I'm telling you anyway!'

'I told you to leave me alone!'

'No, not this time. I want to speak to you!'

'LEAVE ME ALONE!' shouts Antoine. He is getting irritated by her persistance.

'No, this time I need to speak to you and you will listen to me! I don't care if you are mad. You can't win all the time! Stop behaving like a baby and listen to me! You can't always have your way! I exist too, you know!'

Flavie grabs his arm, but Antoine jerks from her grasp and sends Flavie sprawling out on the floor. Surprised, she looks at him. Antoine has kept on working. Flavie tries to get up, she reaches out for him, but Antoine leaves the room without having looked at her once!

* * * * *

Antoine is on holiday. Flavie thinks that it is for the best. She saw him the day after the incident. He did not bother to look at her. Flavie could tell by his eyes that he was still upset, so she stayed away from him.

* * * * *

When Antoine sees Flavie after he comes back, he nods his head in greeting. He is in a very good mood. Each time he sees Flavie, he smiles at her just like nothing has happened. Flavie smiles back, but does not talk to him.

One day she asks him for his help and he obliges. They pass the afternoon cleaning the cupboard. Antoine is in a happy mood and Flavie has such a good time that she forgets the way he sometimes treats her.

Flavie loves him! She loves him too much!!!

* * * * *

'What are you doing for the long weekend?' Antoine asks Flavie point-blank.

'Nothing. Why?'

'Would you like to go camping with me?'

Not able to conceal her surprise and delight, Flavie screams, 'Camping with you! WOW!!'

* * * * *

When he picks her up, she has a box full of food, a suitcase full of clothes and bedding, a big pair of boots, a warm coat, a tuque and mittens.

'We are only going for three days,' Antoine reminds her.

Flavie quivers on the way to the campground, but stays quiet. From time to time, Antoine looks at her but doesn't say a word!

It is very cold outside, the weather is gloomy. Antoine hopes that those three days at the campground will make Flavie understand that they have nothing in common, so that Flavie will stop loving him!

The scenery at the camping ground is gorgeous, but it is too dark for Flavie to notice it. Antoine opens the door of the camper and checks to see if everything is in order. He does not speak to Flavie, who has to manage by herself.

She puts her food in the fridge, puts her suitcase, her blankets and her pillow on the bed that Antoine has pointed out to her. She hangs her coat, her tuque and mittens close to the door. Meanwhile, Antoine has taken his whisky from his pocket and gone outside. He has not said a word to her yet!

It's late, so Flavie puts her pyjamas and her housecoat on and tops it off with her coat before joining Antoine outside. He looks at her and keeps on drinking.

Flavie sits beside him. She's cold.

Antoine sits there drinking and says nothing!

He finishes his whisky, gets up and says, "The bathroom" indicating the latrines outside.

After relieving himself, Antoine goes to bed.

* * * * *

It is dark outside, Flavie is scared. She goes to the latrine and then gets into the camper.

Antoine is sound asleep.

She opens her bed, the sheets do not look clean. She is quite disgusted by other people's filth.

Flavie covers the sheet with her own and then takes the blankets off the bed and puts hers on. After changing the pillowcase, she looks longingly at Antoine, but decides that it is best to go to bed too!

It is only nine o'clock, Flavie cannot sleep. If only there was some light, at least she could read.

Antoine is sleeping and there she is, all alone, sleepless, and very bored.

She looks at him again and wonders what scent his body will release if they make love. Will he taste good? How will it be when he holds her? Love making was so enjoyable with her husband ... So pleasant and delightful!

'Stop that' she scolds herself.

'What else do I have to do?' she answers to herself. 'It's too early to sleep, and he's already sleeping—what is there left for me to do?'

* * * * *

At two in the morning Flavie wakes up. She is cold, she needs to go to the bathroom, but is too scared. If only Antoine had given her a flashlight!

She can't take it anymore, she gets up and tries to wake

Antoine.

'Antoine, I'm cold and I need to go to the bathroom!'

He is too sound asleep to wake up ... so she decides to get into bed with him. It will warm her up. She just has to wake up before him and he won't know the difference!

She lifts the blanket and, slowly, she slides into the bed. Antoine growls, Flavie body is too cold. He turns and puts his arm around Flavie's body. He is so close that she is able to feel his jewels.

'Oh! My God, he's naked!'

Flavie turns her head a little. She wants to know what his body smells like. Flavie likes aftershave lotion on a man's body, but Antoine's body does not smell like anything—no aftershave, no perfume!

Antoine is sound asleep, his body warms Flavie. She finally falls asleep.

When she wakes up, he is already up.

*   *   *   *   *

Flavie puts the kettle on for coffee and to wash up.

When she brings some coffee to Antoine, she asks him what he wants for breakfast.

'Nothing! I only eat once a day, at eight o'clock.'

Flavie eats her breakfast, washes herself and joins Antoine outside.

He is chopping wood, Flavie helps put the logs away.

They do that all day. Flavie helps him, stopping only to eat her lunch. She does not want him to realize that she cannot do it anymore. So, despite her fatigue, she works furiously.

Antoine drinks all day, but he is still able to work. He does not speak, or if he does, it is only mumbling.

At supper time he cooks moose steak, without asking Flavie if she likes that. Flavie does not say anything and eats it.

Then, she does the dishes, puts her pyjamas and her coat on, goes outside and sits.

Antoine has started a fire. He sits there—still drinking his bloody whisky!

Around the fire it's a good place to dream.

Nine o'clock, Antoine finishes his whisky, puts the fire out, and goes to bed.

He has not said a word.

At least, thinks Flavie, even drunk he has enough common sense to put the fire out before going to bed.

* * * * *

That night Flavie is cold. She is also scared, so she goes to sleep with Antoine.

If Antoine finds it strange that she is in his bed, he does not say ANYTHING. He never says ANYTHING!

Today's job is to cut dead trees in the forest. Flavie follows Antoine, but he walks so fast she loses him from time to time.

She tries to hurry up, so she runs. Her foot gets caught in one of the branches on the ground. Flavie falls. She tries to get up, but cannot. The roots will not let go of her tangled foot. She does not have any other choice, she has to ask Antoine for help.

'Antoine, could you come and help me, please? I fell and I can't get up!'

Antoine stops what he is doing and goes toward Flavie.

She looks at him, her eyes begging for help.

Antoine grasps Flavie under her shoulders, puts her on her feet, then bends down and frees her from the roots.

Flavie fixes her pants and thanks Antoine for his help.

Antoine goes back to work without a word.

Flavie looks at him and says to herself, 'How come he never talks?'

The rest of the day goes by without any other incident. Flavie is tired, but she keeps on helping Antoine.

*   *   *   *   *

It will be their last night together. Flavie has worked like crazy to please Antoine and he has hardly spoken to her.

'How come he never says what he thinks? Why he is always so quiet? What he is hiding?'

Tomorrow it will be all over. Flavie must lay her cards on the table tonight.

That night, after washing herself, she puts on perfume.

She also wears her nice pyjamas, but not her housecoat.

She asks him, 'May I comb your hair?'

Antoine gives her a funny look. Flavie shows him her comb.

'May I comb your hair? Is it ok, if I sit on you?'

Since Antoine does not say anything, Flavie sits astride him and starts to comb his hair.

'The weekend is almost over. What will happen between us?'

'There's nothing between us,' grunts Antoine.

'Didn't we just spend the weekend together?'

Antoine does not answer.

Flavie takes a deep breath before saying, 'I love you, but I don't want to live with a man again. I don't want to get married. But I wouldn't mind having an adventure. We could see each other, spend time together, but not live in the same apartment. I am finally free and I enjoy being free. The only condition is—even though we live apart, we have to be faithful. I do not believe in sleeping around.'

Antoine raises his eyes and shouts, 'I am not interested in an affair!'

'It will not really be an affair—we will be a couple that love each other, but would not live together. We will have the best of both worlds!'

Antoine is fixing his eyes on her. At that moment, Flavie feels something. 'My God!' she says to herself. 'One day, I will be his wife! I feel it! The moment he fixed his eyes on me, I felt it! I did!' Because she is not very sure, she does not tell Antoine.—Does he love her?—Sometimes it feels like it and sometimes not.—If he does not like her, how will he become her husband?—Will he love her one day?—Is he her destiny?—Normally, when she gets a feeling about something, it happens—but this time ... will it?

Coming back from her daydreaming, Flavie notices that Antoine was talking to her. She apologizes and asks him to repeat what he was saying.

Antoine takes a deep breath and, impatiently, he pours out, 'I'm 54 years old, I've been divorced twice, separated once, I have three children. I'm through with women.' Putting his hand on his vest, he carries on, 'I like to drink! I've been drinking since I was this high. My step-father was very strict with me and he also drank. I started when very young. It was my way to survive!'

'I know,' acknowledged Flavie. 'You like to drink—that does not bother me! I know you don't have much time to give to me. I'll be satisfied with what little time you have for me. I don't need much—just that you love me. I don't need a beautiful house, jewellery, furs—I just want somebody to love me! I want someone to tell me that he's hungry for my love and anxious to explore the innermost parts of my body.'

'I am not interested! I like my freedom!' he yells back. 'I've been working since I was very young. I never stopped working. I'm always working—I don't have time to give to you! Work and booze, that's all I have time for! Women—I've had lots of women—I don't want women!—I've had enough of women!'

He grabs Flavie by her waist and forces her to get up. And, without another word, he stands and leaves for bed.

* * * * *

Even though Flavie is cold, she does not get into Antoine's bed that night.

'Why can't he love me? Am I stupid to love him? He drinks and he always gets so mad! But he also has good qualities! Will I ever be able to tame that wild stallion?'

Flavie turns so she can examine him. Antoine is sound asleep. She thinks that he is so comely! She still does not know what color his eyes are!

The next day when she wakes up, Antoine is cleaning the camper.

Flavie boils some water, eats her breakfast, then asks Antoine to leave because she wants to wash herself and get dressed.

'You wash yourself too much,' he says laughing. 'You will make a good meal for the bugs.'

After she is finished, Flavie goes to Antoine. He is washing his blue truck.

'Why does your truck look different from other people's trucks?'

Puzzled, Antoine looks at her.

'Yes! it has a horn,' she points out. 'I've never seen a truck with a horn!'

Antoine starts to laugh and keeps on cleaning his truck.

'Is there anything you would like me to help you with?' asks Flavie, seeing that he seems happy.

'You could clean the camper, if you want. It needs a good scrubing.'

Flavie spends the day cleaning the camper while Antoine finishes cleaning his vehicle.

Then, Antoine walks into the woods to see if everything is alright. When he is done with that, he goes into the camper.

He looks at Flavie while he exclaims, 'My God, you did a very good job!'

'Thank you,' says Flavie, surprised.

It is the first time he has complimented her! There may be hope yet!!!

* * * * *

Tuesday morning, Flavie comes to work with an eye that is half closed. Indeed, because she had washed herself too much while camping, she was bitten by mosquitoes.

Antoine sees that and thinks that it is funny.

'Didn't I tell you not to wash so much?'

'Don't laugh at me. It hurts. I cannot open my right eye!'

The next day, Antoine brings her some cream. As he is about to put it on Flavie's eye, she says, 'Wash your hand before you do that! I don't know where they've been!'

Antoine is not happy with what Flavie has said. He thinks her recommendation is unnecessary, so he screams, 'Do you want it to stop hurting or not?' After washing his hands he applies the cream to her eye.

Flavie sighs with relief and says, 'Thank you, that feels good!'

Antoine gives her the cream and recommends her to put it on her eye three or four times a day.

Antoine can be so nice at times!

*   *   *   *   *

Flavie likes Antoine for his beautiful eyes, but she also likes him because he reminds her of a wild stallion. She loves horses! She will do anything for Antoine's love!

She writes poetry that she hides in his shoes. Laughing, she calls them "Magic Shoes."

The Wise Man and the Fool

There once was a man who worked all the time!

As soon as he finished his job, he would work on the side.

Work! Work! Work! That's all he had time for!

He liked to go camping, but he never had time to go!

Money! Money! Money! He always needed money!

Days went by, year passed, and all you saw was him working and working!

No job was too big or too small.

You only had to ask for his help and he would say 'yes'!

One day a Wise Man asked him, 'Why do you work all the time?'

'I need money. I have to pay my bills!'

'Why don't you take the time to relax and enjoy yourself?'

'One day, one day I will!'

'There is that woman,' said the Wise Man, 'she is in love with you! Why don't you ask her out?'

'I have no time for women!'

'She is a very nice girl!'

'Entertaining a woman will take too much of my time!'

'She might be good for you.'

'I really don't care!'

'Only a fool wouldn't take a chance to be happy. Are you a fool?'

The man did not answer. At this the Wise Man left.

The man kept on working, never taking the time to enjoy life.

He never took the time to go camping, took no time for love, working was all that mattered for him.

And one day the man realized that, unfortunately, he was indeed a fool! But it was too late.

Because only a fool would not take time for happiness!

Only a fool would not have time for love!

FC

A Man and His Bottle

There once was a man who liked to drink.

Every day, after work, he went to the bar.

Booze was his life! Booze was his pleasure!

The man was happy. Happiness is doing what you like!

The man would hold his bottle in his hands, just like one would hold a woman.

Night after night he would let his fingers dance slowly up and down his bottle, caressing it.

One day, to his surprise, the bottle spoke to him:

'Why do you touch me so gently? Don't you have someone to love?'

'No,' replied the man, 'I don't have a woman. I am happy just the way I am!'

'Happy!' shouted the bottle, 'how cas someone be happy drinking! You can't tell me that you are happy!'

'I alone am responsible for my own happiness. Leave me alone... let me be!'

The bottle never spoke again. The man kept on drinking.

But he never looked at the bottle again—

Never passed his fingers tenderly over the bottle.

His fingers never again danced or caressed the bottle.

Because, since the bottle had asked him if he was happy... he was not so sure any more...

Can happiness be found in a bottle full of booze?

FC

The Magic Shoes

A man kept finding poems in his shoes—

An envelope and a message on green paper.

'Why?' he always asked himself.

'Who would write such beautiful poems?'

'And why to me? Do I have magic shoes?'

He looked around and saw three women. One was pretty, the other attractive, but the last one rather homely.

He went out with the pretty woman, but all she did was talk about herself. She was only interested in her own person.

'It can't be her. Not once did she acknowledge me.'

The next day he asked the attractive woman if she would like to go out with him.

But she was scatterbrained. She would say things that did not make sense, would laugh for no reason, and was incapable of holding a conversarion.

'A woman like that cannot write such beautiful poems!'

Next was the third woman. He looked at her and said to himself, 'This woman is too plain, she could not write beautiful poems!'

So he never asked her out.

One day she moved away. His shoes stopped being magic!

If we guide ourselvers only on what the eye can see, we are not really seeing!

But if we took the time to look within our hearts, we would see that beauty is not at the surface, but inside each of us.

Happiness is knocking at your door!

Do you have magic shoes?

FC

But Flavie notices that Antoine is not happy with the poems. There won't be any more magic shoes.

* * * * *

Because he has stopped smoking, Antoine keeps either a toothpick or a straw in his mouth at work and drinks a lot of coffee—all to keep his mind from thinking about it.

When Flavie invites him to go have a coffee with her after work, he always answers he does not have time.

One day they both finish working at the same time. Antoine stops and looks at Flavie. She thinks, 'He will surely ask me for coffee!'

But Antoine turns around and leaves without saying anything.

Flavie is sad!

* * * * *

She needs to know. This morning Flavie gets up early, puts on make-up and her new dress, and goes to the Sunset.

Antoine is surprised to see her so early in the morning. He says, 'Good morning,' and keeps on working.

'May I speak to you?' asks Flavie.

'Shoot!'

'Do you think that, one day, you and I ... we will be ... a couple?'

Antoine sighs with impatience and lets his mop drop on the floor.

Flavie, speaking gently, asks him to calm down. 'Stay calm, will you? Look at me, I *am* calm.'

Antoine looks furiously at her and yells, 'I don't want an affair!'

He leaves the room.

Flavie shouts back, but Antoine can't hear her, 'I want more than that! I want to be your wife!'

Since she has convinced herself that Antoine would be her husband, she always thinks about them getting married. She has accepted that fate and she is ready to give up her freedom. So long as Antoine loves her!!! Even though she has offered to become his mistress, it will never happen. Flavie is from the old school—she will not sleep around. First, she has to be in love; secondly, she has to be certain it will last. Yes, Flavie loves to make love. She likes it a lot. It has been a long time! And love is like a box of chocolate—once you open the box and taste one, you cannot stop. The next thing you know, you have eaten it all. The best thing with the box of love is to keep it close. It is better that way than to stay hungry once you have tasted it again. The only guarantee—and for Flavie that means—marriage!!!

Flavie is very opened when talking about sex, but she remains old-fashioned when comes the time to do it. She cannot help who she is!!!

✳ ✳ ✳ ✳ ✳

Flavie knows that she must stop loving him, but how can she when he is always there? She could stop her volunteer work at The Sunset, but she likes working with the elderly—and she is not still ready to wean herself off of Antoine. She loves him too much!!!

She tries to stay away by avoiding him and hardly speaking to him!

But if, for some reason, he smiles at her, she thinks there is hope. So she comes up with the idea of buying him something. He is like a wild horse in need to be tamed.

What does he drink? Flavie is at the liquor store, she is walking down the aisles. There are so many different kinds! What does he like to drink? How much will all that cost?

She asks at the counter if they have gift-certificates. There, she has got herself a gift.

Now she must have a reason. His birthday! But Flavie does not know when it is. She has to find something else. His saint's birthday! No, Saint-Antoine is only in two months! What should she do? 'Ah, who cares! I'll buy a birthday card and wait for his reaction.

She buys the card and writes, *"One day soon ... "*, and she puts the gift-certificate in it. When she gets a chance, she sneaks into the locker room, finds Antoine's coat, and slips the card inside his pocket.

If Antoine has seen the card, he does not mention it!

Flavie would like him to react, maybe to respond by

saying, 'It is not my birthday,' or to say thank you—but, no, he says ... NOTHING

NOTHING!

He acts like he has not received the card or the gift-certificate. Nothing!

He asks for a week off to go hunting. Flavie buys him another gift-certificate and includes a note, *"If you could only give us a chance ..."*

Again ... nothing!

She cannot take it anymore. She dares to ask him. 'What is the matter with you, Mister Dubeau? Don't you like my presents?'

He shouts at her, 'Don't buy me any more gifts!'

So Flavie stops giving him gifts for a while.

* * * * *

Christmas is coming! In an art boutique Flavie admires a sculpture. It is a white horse with some black spots. He is beautiful, gracious, stylish—just like a wild stallion. It reminds her of Antoine. 'I have to buy that for him,' she convinces herself. 'But that would provoke him; didn't he say, "No more presents?" A gift-certificate from the liquor store with the card (since he likes to drink) should mellow him out.'

That night, she writes him a poem and puts it in the card.

Antoine,

You are like a wild stallion!
You are elegant,

Your eyes are beautiful,
And your hair, like a horse's mane,
Dances with the wind!

You are intelligent!
So intelligent that you are never going to get caught!
So wild that you can't be tamed!

Like a wild stallion
You are free.
Every Friday you run away
In the forest
Where you are free to be yourself!

If I was your mare,
I would not be able to run like you
Because
I am not fast enough
To follow you!

I don't have your grace!
I am not pretty,
I don't have your splendid eyes
And
My hair is like straw.

If I wanted to follow you
You would have to leave me behind
Because
If you stopped to help me, like you always do,
You would be in big trouble!
The wolves would attack you!
What a pity
To lose such a magnificent horse like you!

FC

Surely Antoine will thank her, but he says NOTHING! absolutely NOTHING!

* * * * *

Josiane tells her one day, 'Flavie, don't you think it's about time you had a boyfriend?'

Flavie starts to cry.

'A boyfriend! How do you think I could have a boyfriend? I'm too old. Who will want me?'

'Come on, you're not that old! I'll find a man for you.'

'No thank you! I love somebody and he does not love me.'

'Come on! There are lots of men, you know!'

'Maybe, but I just want him.'

'Do I know him? Does he know that you love him?'

'Yes, I told him!'

'Are you crazy! Never tell a man that you love him! A man needs to be the one who takes the first step!'

'It's too late, I already told him!'

'Flavie, do you want my advice? Forget about this man. He does not deserve you. Let love come to you!'

'If I can't have him, I don't want anybody else!'

* * * * *

When Flavie works again, Josiane insists on knowing who the man is that Flavie loves so much. But Flavie refuses to tell her.

Josiane promises she won't tell anyone, but Flavie knows too well that there is no such thing as a secret to Josiane—unless it be an open secret.

'Please!' Josiane begs. 'I won't tell. I promise!'

Flavie takes a deep breath and finally tells Josiane, 'I can't! He does not love me, so what difference does it make whether you know him or not.'

'I promise I won't tell!'

'I just can't!'

Flavie decides to leave the room without looking at Josiane.

* * * * *

'Flavie, it's New Year's Eve. Euclide, Josiana and I are bringing you to the bar.'

'A bar? Are you crazy, Yvette? I don't drink booze!'

'So what?' replies Josiane. It's the best place to meet men.'

'A man! What do you want me to do with that?'

'Come on! You can't spend the rest of your life alone!' adds Yvette. 'Without my Eugene, I don't know what I'd do!'

'Why would I want to be bothered with another man? The two that I had before were more than enough!'

Looking at Euclide, Yvette asks him, 'Don't you have a cousin who is not married?'

'I can't go out with him! I don't know him!' Flavie objects.

'My sister-in-law,' remarked Euclide, 'found her husband by answering an add in the newspaper.'

'And I,' says Josiane, raising her voice, 'I found mine on the Internet.'

'I cannot go out with somebody I don't know, especially not someone from the Internet!' replies Flavie, shocked by their suggestions.

'Why not?' Josiane cries out.

'Because I know too well what those men want ... I'm sorry but ...'

To that Euclide quickly tells her, 'It's not always about sex!'

'With AIDs and all those diseases! No thank you! I'm too scared! As for me ... I have to be in love ... and I prefer to be married before ... I sleep with a man!'

'If you won't go out with guys, how do you expect to ever get married again?'

'Euclide is right,' acknowledges Josiane.

'I'm ok the way I am!' Flavie insists.

'Your tramp,' adds Yvette, 'is at the bar every Saturday— and specially on New Year's Eve.'

'Every Saturday?'

'I see that you're starting to think about it—'

'Well, what should I wear if I decide to go? And I don't want to be there too long!'

* * * * *

Finally, the big day arrives. Everybody looks good in their party clothes. Flavie looks great. She chose to wear a long black dress. She had her hair done and put on make-up.

'Antoine Dubeau,' she say to herself, 'here I am!'

They find a table. Euclide and his wife go dancing. Josiane and her boyfriend from the Internet spend the night kissing. Yvette and her Eugene argue as usual—that is their way to prove to each other their love.

Flavie sits there, looking at all the people. She wishes she had someone who'd love her too!

'Ah, Antoine, why can't you love me!' she sighs.

Then ... she sees him! Yes, it is him. He has just come in. He is wearing a pink shirt—yes, pink! It seems weird for a man like him!

As he walks into the bar, Antoine stops to speak with many people. He seems happy. Flavie follows his every step. She thinks that he is so handsome standing there with his beer in his hand talking with everybody. He looks like he is having a lot of fun.

Flavie cannot take her eyes off him. She knows he has seen her. She wishes that he will come up to her and ask her to dance.

Suddenly, he leaves the bar. 'No!' Flavie whines. 'He's leaving! Why didn't he come to my table to say hello to me? Even a nod of his head would have been more than enough! Ah! it hurts to be in love!'

As Flavie fells sorry for herself, she sees that he has come back and is standing alone at the bar.

'There's my chance, he's alone,' she tells herself. Bravely, she approaches him and proposes, 'I'll buy you two beers if you sit with me!'

Flavie is surprised when Antoine accepts her proposition. She is happy. Finally, she will be able to talk to him!

Flavie wants to be alone with him, but every minute someone comes to speak to him!

Flavie looks at his hands. Antoine has nice hands! She would like to grasp his them, hold them tight, and kiss his fingers one by one. Antoine is so handsome! Ah, so handsome!!!!

Flavie also is beautiful tonight. But did Antoine notice? She has dressed especially for him. But Antoine says NOTHING to her! He never says ANYTHING!

Noticing that they are finally alone, she tosses, 'Here's twenty bucks. Get yourself some beer!'

Antoine almost falls off his chair when he sees her dive into her bra to retrieve the money. Smiling, he takes the money from her and pretends to leave! Flavie, frightened, holds him by the arm. 'Don't go now! Not after I just paid for your drink.'

'But I have to get my drinks,' replies Antoine with a smile on his face.

'Sorry, I thought I offended you when I dived into my bra. I didn't bring a purse because I was afraid someone would steal it. So I'm carrying my money in my bra.'

While Antoine signals to a waiter, Flavie asks him, 'So, did you like my horse?'

'Yes.'

'Did you like my poem?'

'It was ok, I guess!'

'And my gift-certificate?'

'I still have it.'

The waiter puts the beer on the table. Lifting his bottle, Antoine announces happily, 'Let's drink to my health because today is my birthday.'

'Happy Birthday,' retorts Flavie, clinking her glass of water with his glass of beer.

'This is where I spend my birthday every year.'

'And you have fun?'

'I don't know, I get so drunk that I don't remember anything! I don't even know how I find my way home.'

'It must be the horse in you that helps you to make it safely home.'

'I am not a horse.'

'Maybe not, but you remind me of a wild stallion. You know the horse that I bought you? I bought it because, when I saw it, I said to myself, 'That's Antoine. That horse looks like the stallion who guides the other horses in the wild.'

Antoine gives her a funny look.

Meanwhile, Euclide stops at their table to give Flavie a chocolate bar. He knows she likes them.

'Oh! it's so nice of you, thanks,' Flavie says while she offers a piece to Antoine.

'No, thank you,' he says. 'I ate so much of it when I was young, I don't touch that anymore!'

Flavie introduces Euclide to him, 'He's the cook where I work,' she adds.

'There's quite a crowd tonight!' Euclide mentions as he shakes hands with Antoine. 'I'm having so much fun, but tomorrow—Oh, what a hangover I'll have!!!'

'In my case, I don't know what that is,' answers Antoine. 'I've never had a hangover or a headache in my life.'

'You must have a strong stomach!' Euclide says. At that very moment his wife taps him on the back.

'Come on, let's dance,' she says.

'Ahhh, women! You can't live with them and you can't live without them. Let's go.'

'I know,' Antoine sighs. 'I've known lots of women—beautiful, beautiful women—but now—ah!—I could tell many stories—'

'Do tell," says Flavie.

Antoine looks at her a moment.

'Nah! it would take too long.'

He gets up and goes to get himself another beer.

All night, when nobody is around, Flavie tries to get him to talk, but Antoine shies away, as if the conversation was too heavy for him. He does not ask Flavie any personal questions! Nothing—its like she did not exist.

After a moment, he gets up. Flavie thinks he is going to the bathroom. One hour passes—no Antoine; two hours—still no sign of him ...

Flavie is dismayed! He left without saying 'Good Night!', without saying 'Thank you' and he did not even dance with her! She who had dreamt of this moment all this time; she who wanted him to hold her tight in order to fill her nose with his odour so that when she would close her eyes she could imagine those happy moments—it was her dream—she who loves him so much!!!

*   *   *   *   *

That night in her bed Flavie thinks of Antoine, her Wanderer with beautiful eyes.

'Why is he that way? Why can't he say thank you? Why does he always leave like a thief? Why all that silence? He never tells what he thinks. Who is he, that man? Why all those mysteries? ...!'

Flavie is questioning herself. Why does she love him so much? Is it for his beautiful eyes—for his intelligence? Is it because he reminds her of a wild stallion? She likes horses.

'I love him. From the moment his eyes met mine, I've loved him. Ah LOVE, LOVE, LOVE!'

'The heart has its reasons that reason does not understand! Blaise Pascal, how true you were!'

* * * * *

Antoine is at the liquor store. Flavie saw him going in, so she is waiting for him to come out. Enough is enough! He has to explain himself!

His flask in his pocket, he comes out. He sees Flavie, stops. He looks at her and says hello with his head.

Flavie says, 'Hello' and asks if she can talk to him.

Antoine nods, even though he is anxious to take a sip of his drink. He is thirsty, very thirsty!

Flavie starts by thanking him for having accepted to sit with her at the bar. She tells him that she has been waiting for that moment for a long time.

Antoine smiles.

Flavie takes a deep breath and goes on. There are so many things that she needs to discuss with him, so she says whatever comes first to her head.

She tells him, 'You know, instead of screaming and getting angry, if you would tell us what the problem is, you would not have to erupt like a volcano!'

'I have better things to do than explain my emotions!'

'You never say THANK YOU, isn't it?'

'I'm not that kind of guy, sorry.'

'You also never say GOOD BYE!'

'I don't have time for stuff like that.'

'Why did you leave without telling me good bye the other night at the Wizard?'

'If I remember right, I was not your date!'

'Maybe, but you were sitting with me and you were drinking thanks to me!'

'I can buy my own drinks, thank you very much!'

'But you have to acknowledge that you saved money!'

'If that was what concerned you, I can pay you back!'

And Antoine puts his hand in his pocket.

'No, it's not the money that bothers me, it's the fact that you left without saying good bye. I think that I deserve to be treated better than that. I have always been nice to you. Didn't I risk my life to save yours? Does that not count for something?'

'I am who I am.'

'Well, who are you then?'

Antoine chooses not to answer.

'What kind of man are you? Why are you so afraid of love?'

'I don't need women, I am through with women!'

'Why? Are you gay or—Is it because you can't get it up?'

Antoine glares at her! He has had enough of this foolishness, he does not have to stand there and listen to her. He's thirsty, very thirsty!

Why is there always a woman in his life invariably apt at giving lectures and telling him what to do? Especially Flavie, who is not his girl after all. She has no right to question him. He has never made love to her, has always tried to avoid her! True, she smells good and, at times, she is nice to look at. But God knows—if he has to choose between a woman and the bottle, the bottle always wins.

The bottle is and always will be his one and only mistress. She has been his mistress all along and yet never disappointed him. She was there when he was young; she was there as he grew up; she will always be there whatever happens!

Everything was easy before he knew Flavie—why did she have to come and disturb his life? He does not want to know anything about her! It would have been better for him if he had never met her.

He has had enough! Antoine starts to walk away.

Flavie stops him! She grabs his hand. She finally holds his beautiful hand in her hand.

Antoine looks at her. He is getting fed up with all this silliness.

Flavie holds onto him.

'You're not leaving before I finish talking to you!'

'I've heard and said enough, there's nothing else to say.'

'I'm not finished!' shouts Flavie. 'Like it or not, you will listen to me until I'm done! I love you! Sometimes, I feel like you love me and sometimes I feel that you don't love me! What is your problem? Are you afraid of love? Is it because I'm too old? Am I too ugly? Do I stink? What?'

Antoine shrugs in response.

'Are you scared of falling in love?'

'I'm not interested in you. It's nothing personal! I like my freedom. I'm able to do as I please and I don't need a woman in my life—or in my BED! And, by the way, I'm not gay. I just don't need or want you!'

'Why? I need to know why!'

'I don't love you!'

'You never took the time to know me! What do you know about me?'

'I don't care! I just want you to leave me alone!'

'LEAVE you alone—'

Tenderly, she whispers, 'And I who love you so much!' Tears trickle from her eyes! 'It's too bad you don't love me. You and I together would have made sparkles!!!'

Looking through her as if she had disappeared Antoine does not reply. His hand is on his right pocket patting his flask. He is so thirsty!

Despite everything Flavie now knows that she will never win his love! Antoine loves his mistress too much, that damned bottle—that insatiable mistress who has a hold on him like a cancer that eats his body little by little, and will stop only when death comes!

Try as she might, Flavie will never be able to compete with a rival as important as alcohol. Antoine will never change. NEVER!

What a pity!

Flavie looks right at him and says, 'I didn't want to tell you, but I get premonitions—sometimes I sense things and they happen in real life!'

She adds, 'The moment your eyes met mine, I knew that one day ... I would be your wife.'

'That will never happen!' shouts Antoine. 'I will never marry you!'

'We can't change destiny!' she adds, letting go his hand.

Antoine pats his right pockets and tells her, 'I've got my destiny right here in my pocket!'

Flavie watches him go and sighs. 'Too bad! I could have made him so happy!'

THE END

TABLE OF CONTENTS

PRINTED IN 2013

www.ingramcontent.com/pod-product-compliance
Lightning Source LLC
Chambersburg PA
CBHW051841020726
47502CB00005B/1907